A VISIT TO THE COUNTRY

A VISIT TO THE COUNTRY

by Herschel Johnson • paintings by Romare Bearden

Harper & Row, Publishers

Library of Congress Cataloging-in-Publication Data
Johnson, Herschel.
  A visit to the country / by Herschel Johnson ; illustrations by
Romare Bearden : — 1st ed.
      p.   cm.
  Summary : While visiting his grandparents in the country, Mike
finds an abandoned baby bird, takes care of him until he learns how
to fly, and makes an important discovery about when to let go.
    ISBN 0-06-022849-0 : $.   ISBN 0-06-022854-7 (lib. bdg.) :
$
  [1. Birds—Fiction.   2. Country life—Fiction.   3. Grandparents—
Fiction.]   I. Bearden, Romare, 1911–1988   ill.   II. Title.
PZ7.J63197Vi 1989   87-25083
[E]—dc19   CIP
                                                    AC

TO MY MOTHER

Late one afternoon Mike and his grandfather sat on a hill near the railroad tracks. Mike was visiting his grandparents in the country, and he and Grandpa liked to watch the trains go by. The *Mountain Express* was due any minute.

"Look!" said Mike. "Here she comes!"

"Choooooo-choooooo. Choooooo-chooooooo," wailed the train as it raced along the tracks like a rocket.

Mike and his grandfather waved. The engineer blew the whistle again.

"Choooooo-chooooooo. Choooooo-chooooooo."

They watched the train disappear into the distance.

"Some people are always coming and going," said Grandpa. "But I like it best right here."

"Me too," said Mike.

Early the next morning, after breakfast, Mike and his grandfather went to see Cassie the cow. They cleaned her stall and washed her down. Mike's grandfather tried to show him how to milk Cassie, but every time Mike touched her, she would move around and almost knock the milk pail over.

"That's all right," said Grandpa. "She just has to get used to you."

But Cassie did let Mike lead her out to the pasture to graze.

Next, Mike helped his grandmother feed the chickens and collect the eggs.

"Do you need me to help you with anything else, Grandma?" asked Mike after they had brought the eggs into the house.

"No, I think that's all for right now," said Grandma. "You've been a big help today. Why don't you go outside and play awhile?"

Mike decided to go down to the creek. It was one of his special places. There were always birds and squirrels near the creek. And lots of trees and plants. And the water was filled with crayfish and minnows.

Mike walked barefoot on the slippery rocks in the shallow water near the bank of the creek. He liked the way the cool water felt on his hot feet.

When Mike got tired, he sat and listened to the *swoosh* of the rushing water. And the *zee-zee-zee* of the crickets. And the *harumph-harumph* of the bullfrogs.

Then he heard a tiny *cheep, cheep, cheep* sound nearby. He tried to figure out where it was coming from.

"*Cheep, cheep, cheep. Cheep, cheep, cheep.*"

Mike saw a baby bird lying on the ground. He looked up into the trees, but he couldn't see the nest.

Gently, Mike picked up the baby bird.

"Don't worry," he whispered. "I won't hurt you."

Mike took the bird back to his grandparents' house.

"Look, Grandma," he said. "I found a baby bird. Can we take care of it?"

"Well, we can try," she said.

Mike found a shoe box and filled it with tissues. Then he placed the bird carefully into the box, and put in a small bowl of water.

"What's his name?" asked Grandma.

Mike thought for a minute. "His name is Max," he said.

"Hello, Max," said Grandma.

"*Cheep, cheep, cheep,*" said Max, looking up with his mouth wide open.

"Max is hungry," said Grandma. She went into the kitchen and came back with a cup of milk and an eye-dropper.

"*Cheep, cheep, cheep,*" said Max. "*Cheep, cheep, cheep.*"

Mike filled the eyedropper with milk and watched the drops as they fell into Max's mouth.

Soon Max was full. And quiet.

As the days passed, Mike fed Max strings of raw hamburger. And grapes and cherries that he had peeled.

Max seemed to want to eat all the time. He got bigger and bigger every day. And he got more and more red feathers. Max was a cardinal.

One morning Grandpa came down from the attic.

"Look what I found," he said. He showed Mike an old brass bird cage.

Mike and Grandpa fixed up the bird cage so that it was just like new. Mike put Max inside it.

For the next few days, Max was content to just sit in his cage. But soon he started to hop around and flutter his wings.

"Grandma," said Mike, "I think he's trying to fly."

"Well, we can leave the cage door open," said Grandma, "so that he can get out if he wants to try his wings."

Soon afterward, Max hopped onto the cage door.

"Come on, Max," coaxed Mike. "Don't be afraid. You can do it."

But Max clung to the edge of the cage.

"Look," said Mike. "Do this."

Mike hopped up and down and flapped his arms.

Max looked at Mike.

"Come on, Max," said Mike.

Suddenly, Max took off across the room. He fluttered wildly. He twisted this way and that way, careened toward the sofa, then made a less-than-perfect landing with a soft thud.

"You did it, Champ!" shouted Mike. "You flew!"

Soon Max was flying all around the house. Up and down, all around, from room to room he would zoom.

"Go, Max!" shouted Mike.

Max hardly ever returned to his cage now, except to eat. And to sleep.

Max was also full of mischief.

One Sunday, several ladies came to visit Grandma after church. While they were having their tea, Max spotted the cherries atop one lady's hat. He zipped by and tried to grab the fruit.

"Oh!" shouted the lady. "Something's attacking my hat!"

Max tugged at the cherries, but they wouldn't come off, because they weren't real.

"Get away! Get away!" screamed the lady as she ran around the room.

But Max was persistent. He kept tugging at her hat until he knocked it to the floor.

"Mike! You come here and get this bird this minute," shouted Grandma.

Mike had to keep Max in his cage until the ladies left.

The next day, when Max was flying across the room, he crashed into the picture window.

"Max! Max! Are you hurt?" shouted Mike, running over to the bird.

Mike lifted Max from the floor. Max was breathing hard.

Grandma came over.

"Do you think he'll be all right?" asked Mike anxiously.

"I think so," said Grandma. "Put him back in his cage and let him rest awhile."

Mike put some new paper on the floor of the cage and laid Max on it. Max didn't move.

"He wanted to get outside," said Grandma. "That's why he flew into the window. He didn't see the glass."

Mike looked at Max lying on the cage floor. Then he looked at his grandmother.

"But if he gets outside I'll lose him," he said.

"Well, Max is going to keep trying to get outside," said Grandma. "He's a wild creature."

A couple of days later, Max was back to being his old self—flying all over the house.

Mike was excited to see him flying so well. "Go, Max!" said Mike. Then he remembered Max crashing into the window.

Max zoomed past Mike again. "Go, Max," said Mike. But this time he didn't say it very loudly.

That afternoon Mike put Max into the cage and headed for the creek. When they got there, Mike sat looking at Max in the cage. He looked for a very long time. Then he put his finger between the bars and patted Max's head.

"I'm going to miss you, Champ," said Mike. "You're the best flier in the world.... And you've been a good friend."

Mike opened the cage door, and Max hopped onto it. For a long time Max just sat there and looked at Mike.

Then Max flew away, chirping happily. Mike watched him until he was a red flash in the distance.

"'Bye, Champ!" Mike called. Then he slowly walked back to the house.

The next day, Mike sat with his grandfather on the front porch. They both looked off into the woods. It was a bright, clear day, and the countryside seemed to burst with life. The crickets and birds and bullfrogs made more of a fuss than usual. Even the trees seemed to stretch a bit more toward the sun. But Mike still missed his friend Max.

"Do you think Max will ever come back?" Mike asked his grandfather.

"Well, you never know," said Grandpa. "He might come back for a visit. Birds are always coming and going."

"Just like people?" asked Mike.

Grandpa laughed. "Just like people," he said.

Mike and his grandfather were silent for a while. Then they heard the sound of a faraway train whistle. "*Chooooooo-choooooo. Choooooo-choooooo.*"

"It's the *Mountain Express*," said Mike.

"Right on time," said Grandpa. "Feel like taking a look?"

"You bet."

As Mike and his grandfather hurried toward their favorite hill near the railroad tracks, the sounds of the forest seemed to get even louder, and the sun sparkled like a big gold coin. Suddenly, a cardinal darted past them. The bird turned, swooped close to Mike and his grandfather, then zoomed into the forest.

Mike jumped up and down excitedly. "Go, Max! Go!"

Romare Bearden
(1911–1988)

Painter, experimenter with new media, mentor to a generation of young artists, and at one time a songwriter and baseball player, Romare Bearden was one of America's preeminent artists and was considered our foremost collagist. In a single decade he produced 342 collages, 128 oils on paper, 24 drawings, 25 prints, 5 tapestries, 4 murals, and mosaics and assorted other works, including book jackets and quilts. Awarded the National Medal of Arts in 1987, he was termed "the pictorial historian of the black world, especially in the South." But Bearden insisted that his subject was all of America. "Except for the American Indian, everybody who came here or was brought here becomes, starting with the second generation, four things: part Anglo-Saxon, part Indian, part frontiersman and part black. These are the roots that form American culture."

Born in Charlotte, North Carolina, on September 2, 1911, Romare Bearden lived most of his life in the East. After a childhood in Pittsburgh and New York's Harlem, he attended Boston University and New York University, where he majored in mathematics and began to prepare for medical school. Drawing cartoons for the *Afro-American*, a local black weekly, he discovered that he wanted to be an artist, not a doctor. After studying at the Art Students League, he became one of the first to move into what would become New York's downtown artistic community. But Bearden always remembered his roots in the South, and in *A Visit to the Country*, one of his last works (and his only children's book), he evokes the colors, rhythms, and feelings of his past with the loving eye and free hand that come only from long memory and deep emotion.

Romare Bearden died in New York City on March 12, 1988.